My Spring Fling

The Friends to Lovers Series

by

Reba Bale

Table of Contents

Copyright

About This Book

It was supposed to be a vacation romance...until the woman she fell in love with becomes her new nanny!

Margo isn't normally one for flings. Between being a single mother and running the marketing department at a large corporation, she's too busy to breathe let alone take time for herself. But when her seven-year-old daughter goes to stay at her father's for Spring Break, she decides to do something she's never done before – take a solo vacation.

Amelia just finished grad school and to celebrate, she visits an all-inclusive adults-only resort in Mexico. She was planning to decompress and figure out what she wanted to do with the rest of her life, until she meets Margo. The two women have a hot affair, then they say goodbye forever. Until the day that Amelia answers an ad for a summer nanny job and comes face to face with her Spring Fling – and her precocious daughter.

Falling in love with the hot young nanny is a terrible cliché, but that doesn't stop Margo from wondering if Amelia's place in their family can become permanent.

"My Spring Fling" is book nine in the "Friends to Lovers" romantic novella series. Each book in the series is a standalone story featuring an LGBT couple making the leap from friends to lovers and looking for their "happily ever after". If you like steamy but sweet romances with lots of snark, download this lesbian romance today.

Be sure to check out a free preview of Reba Bale's lesbian romance "The Divorcee's First Time" at the end of this book!

Dedication

For everyone who had a vacation fling and thought, "Wouldn't it be great if fate brought us back together again?"

Join My Newsletter

Want a free book? Join my newsletter and you'll receive a fun subscriber gift. I promise I will only email you when there are new releases or special sales, usually twice a month.

Visit my newsletter sign-up page at bit.ly/rebabooks[2] to join today.

---

2. https://bit.ly/rebabooks

Prologue—Amelia

Three months ago...

"I wish I didn't have to go home tomorrow."

"Me too."

I squeezed my arm around Margo's waist, my fingers sinking into her soft flesh. The moonlight coming through the open balcony door lit up her face, almost making her look like an angel.

I'd come to this resort in the Mexican riviera to celebrate my recent graduation from grad school. With my newly minted master's degree in elementary education, I'd already lined up a job as a fourth-grade teacher starting in the Fall. I figured I'd take a little solo trip to unwind from the pressures of school, then move up to Seattle and find a summer job to tide me over until my teaching gig started.

After six years of college and grad school, I was exhausted. I'd worked full-time throughout school, as well as taking a full course load. I hadn't had a vacation since I graduated high school.

A friend had told me about this adults-only all-inclusive resort in the Mexican Riviera, and while it was expensive, I was able to use airline miles to bring the cost down to something I could better afford.

I figured I'd spend a week in blissful solitude, laying on the beach soaking up the rays and drinking frothy concoctions with little umbrellas in them. I'd just broken up with my last girlfriend a few months ago, so having a vacation romance never even crossed my mind.

On my second day here, I'd looked over to see someone settling into a lounger next to me on the beach. I'd taken one look at the curvy body trying to burst out of a conservative one-piece bathing suit and felt a jolt of lust. Then the woman had looked over at me, dark brown eyes snagging mine, and I'd felt something that felt more like love.

It was ridiculous of course. Love at first sight wasn't a real thing. I'd resolved to control my overactive imagination. Clearly what I was feeling was only lust. Intense lust.

I wasn't alone in the attraction. Margo and I had started talking, and within hours I was somehow following her to her cabana. The minute we closed the door we were on each other, giving into the strong heat that had been building between us all afternoon. Underneath that heat was fire.

I spent the rest of the week exploring all the curves of her body – when she wasn't exploring mine.

We'd laid on the beach, eaten several great meals, gone swimming and snorkeling, but more than anything, we'd had sex. Incredible sex. Marathon sessions where I ate her pussy like it was my job and Margo used her fingers and tongue on me until I was screaming beneath her, begging to come.

I'd had a few sexual partners over the years, but it had never been like this. Nothing had ever felt so explosive. So perfect.

But Margo and I had agreed right at the beginning that this was only a vacation fling. We never traded last names, never talked about our families or careers or shared where we lived. We kept our conversations at the surface level, content to let our bodies do the talking.

Maybe on some level we knew that if we shared anything personal it would be too hard to say goodbye. We might not have talked about our feelings, but one thing was clear: I wasn't alone. I could tell that Margo was as overwhelmed by the strength of our connection as I was. I could see it in her eyes, and in the unguarded expressions she had when she didn't know I was watching her.

And now it was our last night together. I was here for two more days, but Margo was flying out in the morning. I had a feeling the resort wasn't going to be the same without her next to me.

Margo turned onto her side, her brown eyes serious. My gaze traced her straight blonde hair, mussed from my fingers, and her smooth face, golden from our many hours in the warm sun. She had the cutest little upturned nose, which softened the look of her face. I knew she was ten years older than me, but you'd never be able to tell by looking at her youthful face.

"I've really enjoyed our time together, Lia" she said softly. "I've never...it's never been like this before. Not with anyone, ever."

I stroked her cheek with my fingers. "I know. I feel the same. If only..."

She pressed a finger against my mouth, silencing me.

"There's no sense in wondering what could have been," she said. "This isn't some movie where people fall in love on vacation, and everything magically works out for them to live happily ever after together."

"That's too bad," I said sadly, even though I knew she was right. "I've always loved those movies."

Margo

The doorbell rang as soon as I sat down to pee. Didn't it always?

"I'll get it," my daughter Skyler yelled.

"Wait for me," I yelled back, finishing quickly so I could wash my hands and answer the door.

No doubt it was the new nanny the agency was sending over for us to interview. I really hoped Skyler liked her. We'd had a hell of a time finding a nanny that my daughter liked, and I was running out of options with school ending this week. I would have started my search earlier, but I thought last year's nanny was returning for the summer. Unfortunately, she'd decided to take another job at the last minute.

I rushed to the front of the house, unsurprised to see that Skyler had already opened the door despite the fact that I'd told her a million times not to do that unless an adult was with her.

"What have I told you about opening the door without me?" I chided my seven year old.

She turned to give me her innocent face, the one she affected when she wanted to pretend that she didn't know what I was talking about. Skyler was my mini-me, with dark blonde hair and features that matched my own at that age. Her bright blue eyes and exuberant personality were the only things she'd inherited from her father.

I heard a soft gasp and turned my attention from my daughter to the woman standing on my doorstep.

I took in her slim but curvy body, long, curly red hair, green eyes, and a nose splattered with freckles. Three months ago I'd kissed every single one of them. Repeatedly.

"Lia? What on Earth are you doing here? How did you know where I live?"

I saw a flash of hurt cross her face at my harsh tone. I was confused. We'd never exchanged last names. Never even shared what states we lived in. Had she searched my wallet while I was sleeping or something? Oh my God, was she a crazy stalker? She seemed emotionally stable when we were in Mexico, but you never really know...

"Margo? You're Margaret Langley?" she asked, looking confused.

"Yes."

Skyler grabbed the hem of Lia's shirt, drawing her attention back to where she preferred it: on herself. My daughter was nothing if not self-confident.

"Are you the new nanny?" Skyler asked hopefully.

"My name is Amelia," she confirmed. "The nanny agency sent me over to meet you. You must be Skyler."

My daughter smiled.

"Yes, I'm Skyler. I have a question for you: which mutant ninja turtle is the best?" she asked.

"Leonardo," Lia answered without hesitation.

My daughter pressed one finger to her lips, thinking.

"What's your favorite ice cream flavor?"

Lia squatted to be on eye level with my daughter, settling in for her interrogation. It made her skirt rise on her thighs in a way that made me have thoughts that were not appropriate when my daughter was in the room.

"Peanut butter chocolate."

"Good choice," Skyler said approvingly. "Mine is rocky road."

"Also a good choice," Lia said.

"Which do you like better? Dogs or cats?"

"Dogs," Lia said. "Although I like cats too, just not as much as dogs."

"Do you like video games?" Skyler asked.

"Yes, but I also like to be outside, especially in the summer."

"What's your favorite color?"

"Purple."

"Mine too. One more question," my daughter said, pausing dramatically. "Have you ever kissed a boy?"

Lia's gaze shot up to mine before returning to my daughter.

"Yes. A long time ago."

"Was it gross?"

"Totally." Lia gave her an impish smile.

"Okay, you're hired," Skyler said decisively.

I was impressed that Lia was the first nanny applicant who had answered Skyler's questions to her satisfaction. If only I didn't know what it felt like to have her come her brains out while straddling my face. Maybe then this would feel less awkward.

"Isn't that decision up to your mom?" Lia asked.

Skyler looked back at me for the first time.

"Mommy, I like this one. Let's keep her."

"Honey, I need to talk to Lia alone for a few minutes."

"She said her name is Amelia," Skyler said, her tone clearly conveying that I was an idiot.

"Lia is my nickname," my vacation fling explained patiently. "Kind of like your mom's real name is Margaret but some people apparently call her Margo."

"Oh yeah, that makes sense," Skyler said. "I don't have a nickname. Everyone just calls me Skyler."

"Understood," Lia told her in a serious tone.

We all stood there awkwardly for a long moment.

"Why don't you go watch one of your shows, Skyler," I suggested. "You can have thirty minutes of screen time."

"Whoo hoo!" she cheered. "See you soon Amelia."

"It was nice to meet you, Skyler."

As my daughter ran off, Lia stood up and met my gaze.

"Well, this is a really weird coincidence," she said, her face shuttered. "How have you been?"

"I'm fine," I answered, keeping my voice neutral. "I didn't know you lived in Seattle," I said.

"I just moved here, but I didn't know you lived here either," she said.

Of course she was right. We'd never shared anything too personal. I'd insisted that we keep everything surface level when we were together. My feelings for Lia had been so strong that I knew if I'd gotten to know her I wouldn't be able to let her go. I'd never had a vacation fling before, or any kind of fling really, but I understood that they were supposed to be temporary, no matter how strong the feelings seemed to be when you were together.

"You never told me you had a kid," Lia said, a slight note of disapproval in her voice. "It seems like that would have come up somehow."

I don't know why I hadn't. Maybe I was just enjoying being a woman for once, not a mom. As much as I loved my daughter, that vacation without her had been good for my soul. Plus I hated those women who only identified themselves as moms, as if that was their life's purpose.

Lia suddenly looked horrified. "Oh my God! Are you married? Is that why you were so close-mouthed about your personal life?" She looked around like someone was going to jump out and attack her. "Do you have a partner?"

"No, of course not," I protested. "I'm not married or dating anyone. I wouldn't have been with you if I was with someone else."

Her face smoothed.

"Well, obviously this nanny thing isn't going to work, given our history. I'll tell the agency to send over another applicant."

Lia swayed towards me like she wanted to kiss me, or maybe give me a hug the way she'd done when I'd said goodbye to her at the resort, but then she straightened her spine. I lifted my hand, then lowered it, resisting the temptation to touch her.

"Good luck with your search, Margo. Tell Skyler I said goodbye."

Before I could say anything, she rushed out the door and disappeared.

Amelia

I ran out to my car, drove two blocks, then pulled over to calm down. My mind was racing, my emotions mixed. Ever since she'd left Mexico I'd dreamt of running into Margo somehow. I knew it was a ridiculous fantasy, but in my imagination, fate brought us back together, then we fell into each other's arms and picked up where we left off in Mexico.

Little did I know that fate had a sick sense of humor.

The look of horror on Margo's face had been like a punch in the gut. So had the adorable little girl. Margo had never once even hinted that she had a kid. I guess it wouldn't have made a difference, since we'd agreed to a vacation fling, but I wouldn't have been so fixated on her afterwards if I'd known that she was a mom.

I never, ever dated women with kids. It was too awful when you broke up. Losing a lover was one thing, but losing someone who was like a son or daughter to you was something else. One time was all it took for me to know I could never do that again. And it hadn't taken long for me to realize that I would fall for little Skyler as fast as I'd fallen for her mom. The kid was freaking adorable.

After letting the agency know that I wasn't a good nanny match for the Langley family, I headed to a little coffee shop called Morning Jolt that was a few blocks from my new apartment. Even though I'd only been living in this neighborhood for a few weeks, the barista, Hannah, greeted me by name.

"How's it going Amelia?" she asked, giving me a friendly smile.

She was about my age, curvy with blue hair and lots of tattoos. I might have been interested in her if she was single. At least I would have been interested pre-Margo. I knew Hannah was a lesbian because I'd seen her girlfriend in here flirting with her. She looked like the opposite of Hannah, dressed in conservative clothes for some office job, but they were adorable together.

"I'm not bad," I said, pointing at a giant banana nut muffin. "Can I get a muffin and a black coffee please?"

"Sure thing. Hey, how was your job interview? It was today right?"

Hannah should be a bartender. Despite her grunge rocker look, she was kind and empathetic and super interested in her customers. With how crowded this place was all the time, I couldn't believe she remembered my offhand comment a few days ago about having a job interview today.

"It didn't go well," I sighed. "I loved the kid, and she liked me, but you'll never believe it, the mom was an ex. Well, kind of an ex. We had a torrid affair a few months ago on vacation. I never expected to see her again, but there she was. I didn't even know she lived in Seattle."

"Wow, that's a weird coincidence."

She slid my coffee across the counter, and I tapped my phone against the scanner to pay.

"Yeah, it was totally awkward, especially when I saw the look of horror on the mom's face," I shared. "I think she thought I was stalking her or something before she realized that I was there about the nanny job. She didn't even ask me any questions, just stared at me while the kid interviewed me."

"That's rough. Well, maybe there's a better nanny job out there?"

The agency says that they don't really have any other summer jobs open right now, so I'm going to have to figure out a plan B I guess, just in case they don't come up with something."

"I can always see if the manager has any shifts open here," she offered. "I'm pretty sure he's looking for some on-call folks to fill in shifts when people are off."

"Oh thanks Hannah, that would be great."

I mean sure, I have a master's degree, I should totally pour coffee, I thought to myself sarcastically. I shook my head, trying not to be discouraged. I had a great job waiting for me when school started, I just needed something to help me pay the bills over the summer. I probably shouldn't be discounting a job here at the coffee shop. At least it was easier than being a nanny, and close to home too.

Taking my coffee and muffin, I found a table in the corner and opened my battered laptop, ready to look for other job options. A few minutes later, my phone dinged with a text from my contact at the nanny agency.

Nannies Inc.: *Hey Amelia, it's Gail from Nannies Inc. I just got a call from Margaret Langley, and she'd like to hire you. I guess the interview didn't go as bad as you thought.*

Me: *No thanks. I appreciate the offer, but that placement isn't going to be a good fit for me.*

Nannies Inc.: *I'm sorry to hear that. I'll let the client know.*

Me: *Thanks, please let me know if something else comes up.*

I was pretty shocked that Margo wanted to offer me the job. She hadn't even interviewed me, although her daughter had. I didn't know if Margo was really interested in me for the position, or she just didn't want to come off like a jerk after the way she acted when she saw me on her porch. She had to know me being the nanny was a bad idea given our history. There'd been a moment right before I left where we'd almost kissed or something. It would be impossible to keep things professional if we were together on a daily basis.

The next day I received another text from Gail.

Nannies Inc.: *Hi it's Gail. Margaret Langley really wants you for this job. She said her daughter is heartbroken that you turned down the job. The little girl doesn't want anyone else. Mom's offering you a 5k signing bonus.*

Me: *I'm sorry but I can't.*

Nannies Inc.: *She's also offering a month stipend on top of your salary, payable at the completion of your assignment.*

Me: *Thank you for considering me, but I can't.*

Nannies Inc.: *May I ask why? They're offering a lot of money.*

Me: *It's not about the money. It's just not a good placement for me. I'm sure you can find someone more suitable.*

Nannies Inc.: *I'm supposed to ask you what it will take to make you change your mind. Honestly, I think you can ask for almost anything.*

Me: *Nothing. I'm not playing hardball or anything. I just don't want this particular job. It's not a good fit for me. I'm sorry.*

True to her word, Hannah got me hooked up with some relief work at Morning Jolt. Apparently one of the full-time baristas, Camille, was reducing her hours because she was having some success as a science fiction writer, and she wanted more time to write. It helped that, according to Hannah, she'd just moved in with the shop owner, business mogul millionaire Madison Phoenix, so she had a little more freedom to focus on her writing. I'd be filling in for some of Camille's shifts and covering some vacation shifts until the manager found a new full-time barista.

A week later, I was working on a Monday morning when I heard a high-pitched squeal of delight.

"Abigail! It's you!"

I looked up to see Skyler walking in the door, her mother behind her. The little girl looked thrilled to see me as she bypassed the line to race up to the counter, with a huge smile on her face.

"Skyler! We need to wait our turn," Margo called, stepping to the back of the line.

Skyler ignored her, coming to lean against the counter.

"Abigail! I'm so glad to see you again."

"How are you, Skyler?" I asked as I took payment from the guy whose coffee I'd just made. He shot my young friend an indulgent glance.

"I'm good," she said seriously. "I'm going to go to work with my mom today. My mom says since I don't like any of the nannies I hafta come with her, but I need to be very very quiet all day."

"Well, that's nice," I said encouragingly.

"It's going to be sooo boring!" Skyler corrected me, her tone dramatic.

I glanced at the next customer, an older woman who didn't seem too annoyed by my little guest. "What could I get you?"

"I'll take a cappuccino and a blueberry scone please."

"Coming right up, ma'am."

Skyler chattered away while I made the woman's cappuccino.

"I only want you to be my nanny, nobody else, but Mommy says you don't want to work with us anymore."

I looked over my shoulder at her, then glanced towards Margo, who was watching the scene from her place in line. Finishing the drink, I passed it on to the woman and waited for her to tap her phone to pay.

"I don't think I'd be the best nanny for you, Skyler," I said gently. "I'm sure the agency has someone better for you."

"Don't you like me?" Her eyes filled with tears.

The man who'd just stepped to the front of the line looked at me impatiently, clearly having no time for a child's tears.

"It's not that I don't like you. But hold on Skyler, let me help this gentleman first, then we can talk."

Once I'd gotten the man his mocha, the man strode away, and Margo reached the front of the line.

"Lia is working, honey. Quit bothering her and give her your order so we can go to my office."

Skyler stomped her foot. "I don't want to go to work! I want to stay here with Amelia!"

Sensing a tantrum coming on, I walked to the door separating the café from the kitchen.

"Hey Hannah, do you mind if I take a quick break?"

"I'll be out in a sec to cover for you."

"I'll tell you what Skyler, why don't you tell me what you want to drink and then I'll take a break and talk to you if it's okay with your mom."

I glanced at Margo, who nodded and looked a little relieved.

I made a hot chocolate for Skyler while Hannah got a cup of drip coffee for Margo. Grabbing a bottle of water for myself, I followed them to a table. The minute we sat down, Skyler started talking. Margo put her hand on her daughter's shoulder, giving it a little squeeze.

"Honey, let Mommy talk for a minute."

Margo sent me a frazzled look.

"I need you, Lia. Please reconsider taking the job. Skyler has hated every other nanny candidate. Every. One."

Skyler nodded vigorously. "It's true. They were all mean. And one lady smelled funny."

"Just putting my cards on the table, I'm getting desperate. I need someone to help while I'm at work, and I'm out of time. I can't bring Skyler to work every day for three months. Plus she won't stop talking about you."

She looked at me intently. "What do I need to do to make you take the job? Please. I'll do anything."

Margo

I couldn't believe our luck, running into Lia this way. It was ironic that she was working at the coffee shop that was a few blocks away from my office. I hoped I could convince her to change her mind about the nanny job. Skyler had been a nightmare the past few days, whining non-stop about how she wanted Lia. We'd had a couple other nanny candidates and she'd refused to even talk to them because they weren't Lia.

She wasn't normally so difficult, which made the whole situation even weirder. I guess I couldn't blame Skyler though, I'd been obsessed with Lia since the moment I'd laid eyes on her back in Mexico.

I'd spent the entire plane ride back from vacation doubting my decision not to get her contact information and daydreaming about the two of reuniting someday. Once I'd gotten home though, I'd pushed her to the back of my mind. Telling myself that it was just a fling, that I'd never see her again, that I had no way to find her even though I desperately wanted to.

When I saw Lia standing on my front porch, I had to face the reality that I wasn't just obsessed with her. As ridiculous as it sounded, I was also in love with her. And there wasn't a thing I could do about it.

If by some miracle I convinced her to work for me, I needed to keep her at arm's length. I wasn't going to be that weirdo who perved on the nanny, even if I couldn't forget the way her face screwed up in pleasure when she came.

"What do I need to do to make you take the job? I'll do anything."

I'd be glad to pay her in orgasms if that was her price, I thought. Lia's eyes met mine, her pale skin turning pink as she pondered the possibilities. In that moment I knew for sure that she was just as affected as I was.

"Pleeeeease Amelia," Skyler pleaded, holding her hands up in prayer. "I swear I'll be the best kid ever if you save me from a boring summer at my mom's office."

Lia rolled her lips in to suppress a smile.

"I'll get a sign-on bonus?" Lia asked me.

"Yes."

She looked between me and my daughter, considering.

"How about we try it for a week and see how it goes? If it doesn't work, I'll help you find another nanny."

Skyler cheered loud enough to make every head in the place turn in our direction. "Yay! Can you start now?"

"No, I have to finish my shift here at the coffee shop today," she said. "But how about I come over tomorrow?"

My daughter extended her hand to shake. "You've got a deal."

We made arrangements for Lia to come at seven-thirty the next morning, so we'd have some time to talk before I left for work at eight-fifteen. She got there a few minutes early, wearing shorts, a tee shirt, and a pair of battered keds, a hair tie on her wrist. She looked fresh and young, and I felt like a weirdo when my panties dampened at the sight of her in my living room.

Trying hard to focus, I showed her around the house, making sure she had my contact information to put in her phone and giving her a key for when she and Skyler went out.

"Nice place," Lia said as we finished the tour.

"Thank you."

I lived in a large townhouse in one of Seattle's nicest neighborhoods. My ex-husband and I had sold the house we lived in when we'd divorced, and I'd opted to relocate closer to the office since I had Skyler during the week. Fortunately, my job paid very well.

"What kind of work do you do?"

I realized we'd never even shared that level of information in Mexico. Then again, we were pretty busy fucking each other's brains out. And eating seafood.

"I'm the VP of Marketing for Phoenix Software," I said, naming one of Seattle's biggest tech companies.

"Oh, you work for Madison Phoenix?" she said. "That's funny, she owns the Morning Jolt coffee shop too. I guess that makes her both of our bosses."

"Yeah, but she really just bought that place for her girlfriend," I told her. "And also because she didn't want to take a chance of someone else buying the place and depriving her of her favorite muffins. She's very finicky about her food."

Lia laughed softly, and I remembered all the ways she was ticklish. I pressed my thighs together and tried to focus on business. For my daughter's sake, I needed to keep this professional.

"Skyler should be awake soon."

"Does she have any allergies or health conditions?" Lia asked. "Any phobias I should know about?"

I shook my head. "No, I'm really lucky. Skyler is both healthy and fearless."

Just then the girl in question came stumbling out, looking adorably sleepy. She'd slept in later than usual but when she saw Lia she was immediately alert.

"Amelia!" she yelled. "You came!"

My daughter had a voice that really carried.

Lia dropped to her knees, accepting the hug that Skyler offered.

"I promised you I would come, didn't I?"

The sight of my daughter wrapped in Lia's arms was doing funny things to my heart. I pressed my palm against my sternum and drew in a ragged breath.

"I'd better get to work," I said. "I should be home around six o'clock."

"Bye Mommy," Skyler called over her shoulder, uninterested in me now that Lia was here.

I tousled her hair.

"Be good for Lia, okay? Don't badger her for extra screen time and listen to everything she says."

"I will," she promised.

The next two weeks passed quickly. Lia would arrive promptly at eight, and we'd exchange information before I left for work. She texted me midday to let me know how things were going, often including a selfie of her and Skyler doing something fun, like building a fort in the living room or playing at the park. When I got home from work, Lia and I would chat for a few minutes so she could update me on their day, then she would take off for home. I'd spend the rest of the night hearing stories from Skyler about their adventures together.

Every once in a while we'd have some accidental contact: a brush of the shoulders, the meeting of fingers, or lingering eye contact that made me want to wrap my legs around her waist and demand she carry me to bed. And then I'd call myself all kinds of a fool for harboring fantasies that would never come true.

One day she was showing me some pictures of Skyler on her phone, and while we'd huddled in close to watch the screen, our shoulders had touched. I inhaled deeply, getting a whiff of Lia's shampoo. Just the scent of her coupled with an innocent touch had been erotic as hell, and when I'd looked down, Lia's nipples were as hard as mine were.

Every night after my daughter went to bed, I'd close my bedroom door and dream about the adventures I wanted to have with Lia. I knew it was wrong, but I'd close my eyes, picture Lia in whatever outfit she'd worn that day, then slide my hands into my panties and make myself come until I was relaxed enough to sleep. I knew it was wrong, but I couldn't help fantasizing about her.

Lia was strictly professional whenever I saw her, never giving an indication that we'd ever been more than boss and employee. It drove me crazy, wondering if she was still as attracted to me as I was to her. I found myself asking her more questions when we saw each other, trying to prolong our time together.

Things were bound to break sometime.

It was Friday, the second week Lia was working for me, and Skyler was awake before she got there.

"Hey Mommy, can we have pizza tonight?"

I looked up from putting on my make-up. "Sure honey, that sounds good."

Just then the doorbell rang, and Skyler skipped out of the room to answer the door for Lia. When I got to the living room, Skyler was talking excitedly about the pizza.

"It's our favorite place. We always get the vegetarian pizza because Mommy and I think it's best." She lowered her voice like she was telling a secret. "Even though we're not vegetarians, we like it anyway."

"Well that sounds delicious," Lia said indulgently. She sent me a smile that made me inexplicably happy. "Good morning, Margo."

"Good morning, Lia."

"Mommy, can Amelia stay for dinner tonight? Pizza is one of her favorite foods too. She told me yesterday."

Ah, now the sudden desire to have pizza tonight made more sense.

"Oh no, I couldn't impose," Lia protested. "Besides, I'm sure your mom wants to hang out with you before you go to your dad's tomorrow."

My ex-husband got Skyler two weekends a month, plus alternating school breaks. I was lucky. We'd had an amicable divorce, and we were good friends as well as co-parents.

Our marriage ended quietly. There were no big fights, no cheating. It was more that we'd both gradually realized that we weren't in love with each other. I was bisexual, which my ex had known when we got together, but ever since the divorce I'd mostly dated women. So did he, so we liked to joke about comparing notes. He was the one person who'd heard all about my vacation fling with Lia.

"Please Lia, please stay!" Skyler yelled.

"Inside voice," I chastised.

My daughter turned her puppy dog eyes on her nanny in an attempt to get her way. I looked at Lia, trying to determine if she wanted to stay for dinner or not. I didn't want to make her uncomfortable, but on the other hand, I wanted nothing more than to spend some time with her.

These quick drive-bys as we handed off Skyler were killing me. I decided to add my invitation to Skyler's.

"We'd love it if you could stay for pizza Lia, if you're available tonight."

Amelia

"Is she asleep?" Margo whispered.

After a full day together, Skyler and I had dinner with Margo, stuffing ourselves with pizza before heading into the living room to watch "Encanto", a movie I knew for a fact Skyler had already seen about a million times. Not that I minded. I kind of liked it myself.

"Yeah."

We'd started off sitting on the couch together with the little girl in the middle, but somehow Skyler had maneuvered us until I was sitting in between her and her mother. I'd spent most of the night trying to ignore the hum of awareness that seemed to travel between me and Margo like a force field whenever we were together.

Maybe it was my imagination, but I could swear Margo was giving me 'come hither' eyes all night. I'd first seen that look on the beach in Mexico, and it had the same effect then as it did now.

Meanwhile, I had a sneaking suspicion that my ward was engaging in a little matchmaking between me and her mother. Skyler had increasingly been prying into my personal life.

Yesterday we'd been walking along a hiking trail that circled a large lake, stopping occasionally to throw stones into the water when she gave me a speculative look.

"Do you date boys or girls?" she'd started.

She already knew I was single and didn't have children, based on earlier questions.

"I date girls," I said noncommittally.

I knew from my experience student teaching that it was best to be neutral when kids started quizzing you about your life. Even the nosiest kid would lose interest if you were matter of fact in your answers.

Of course Skyler wasn't the average kid.

"My mom dates girls," she shared. "Except for my daddy. He's a boy. Mommy says she likes girls better."

I had a flash of myself sucking on her mom's generous breasts and gave my head a little shake to knock that thought out of my brain.

"That's nice."

"You should date my mom."

"Um. I don't think that would be a good idea," I'd said.

"Sure it would," Skyler argued. "You both don't got a girlfriend, and if you got married you could live at our house. We could make forts and have sleepovers. Then I would have two mommies like my friend Kaitlin. It would be so much fun."

She wasn't wrong, that did sound fun, not that I would admit that to a seven-year-old.

"How about you worry less about who your mother is dating and more about yourself?" I'd suggested, earning me a pouting look.

It was time to redirect. "Hey, is that a heron over there?"

The little girl had taken the change in subject in stride, but when she'd invited me to stay for pizza, I knew she hadn't forgotten her matchmaking ideas. I'd intended to refuse the invitation, but something in Margo's eyes had made me want to stay.

And now here we were, sitting on the couch, close enough that I could feel the heat of Margo's body, with her little girl sacked out against my other side.

"I'm going to carry her to bed," Margo whispered.

"Okay."

She stood up to reach for Skyler, and her hand brushed the side of my breast. I gasped as an electric shot zapped through my body. Our eyes met for a long, heated moment.

"Oh. Um, sorry," Margo said, gathering up her daughter. "Don't go. I'll be right back."

I turned off the television and picked up our glasses to take them to the dishwasher. As I turned around from loading them on the racks, Margo was stalking towards me, intent clear in her eyes.

Before I had any idea what was happening, we flew towards each other, meeting in the middle of the room. Margo's hands rose to my shoulders, my hands going to either side of her face, and our mouths met in a frantic crash of lips and teeth.

The minute our tongues touched, it felt like coming home. I'd missed this so much. I'd missed her. Brief conversations as we passed off her child to each other didn't count.

I lowered my hands to Margo's round ass, palming her cheeks and pulling her pelvis towards mine. I shoved my knee between her legs so she could grind against my thigh, my own core rubbing against her leg, seeking pressure. My nipples hardened painfully against the fabric of my bra.

It had been like this in Mexico too. The minute we touched, my entire body was on fire. And now that I knew her a little better – knew the real her – my feelings were even stronger. It felt like more than a physical thing now. When we finally pulled apart, we were both breathless. My panties were soaking wet.

"What are we doing?" I whispered.

"I don't know," Margo said. "All I know is that I've been dying to do this ever since you showed up on my porch that first day."

She kissed me again, slower this time, but it was just as intense.

"Come to my bedroom," Margo whispered. "I want you, Lia. So much."

My heart was beating so hard I thought it might break through my chest. This was probably a terrible idea, but the past few weeks had been an exercise in deprivation. No amount of masturbating had been able to remove the ache between my thighs that came from being around Margo and not being able to touch her.

"What about Skyler?" I forced myself to ask. "We don't want to confuse her." My voice was thick with need.

"She won't hear us. She sleeps like the dead," she said, kissing me again.

Margo started walking us towards the back hallway, stopping every few steps for us to kiss each other. Our hands roved each other's bodies, touching anything we could reach. By the time we got to the bedroom, I was damn near ready to explode from desire.

She led me into the bedroom, pulling the door shut behind us.

"Please, stay with me, Lia," she said. "We'll get up early and you can go home then. I want you so bad. I've missed sleeping next to you and waking up in your arms."

God help me, there was no way I could say no to that. Not when I felt the same. I was literally burning for her.

"Get naked," I ordered.

She gave me a sultry smile. "You first."

I pulled off my tee shirt, then my bra, releasing my breasts. They were small and pale, the skin above covered with reddish freckles, thanks to my Irish parents. Not that Margo had minded my small size. When we were in Mexico she'd spent hours stroking and sucking on my breasts.

Kicking off my shoes, I pulled down my shorts and panties, glad to be out of the damp fabric.

Margo pulled off the yoga pants and tee shirt that she'd put on when she'd gotten home from work, leaving her in a hot pink satin bra and matching panties.

"That's what you had on under those soccer mom yoga pants?" I teased. "You naughty girl."

She gave me a smile. That was the thing about me and Margo, even though there was a lot of passion between us, we'd also been able to laugh and joke around when we were together. It added a level of fun to being with her that was different from anyone else I'd been with.

Margo unhooked her bra, then shimmied out of her panties. Crooking her finger at me in a silent order to follow, she headed for the bed. She pulled back the comforter, then hopped up right in the middle of the mattress. I followed her, rolling right on top of her to give her a long, deep kiss.

I slid one hand down to dip between her legs, finding her soaked. I explored her folds before slipping a finger deep inside her. I added a second finger and began pumping it in and out, rubbing the heel of my hand against her clit with every pass. Margo pumped her hips, meeting my hand and moaning into my mouth.

I knew exactly what to do. We'd had sex so many times during our week in Mexico, it had been like a graduate level class in how to get Margo off.

"Oh my God, I've missed this," she gasped when we finally broke apart. "You're so fucking sexy."

I lowered my head, nipping along her collar bone. Her hands stroked my naked back.

"I'll tell you what," I said. "I'm going to eat you out, then I want you to fuck me with your fingers."

When we'd been in Mexico, Margo had generally been content to follow my lead, which was good, because I tended to be a bit bossy in the bedroom. But tonight I was seeing a different side of Margo. She stuck her arm out, reaching for the drawer of the bedside table.

She gave me a wide, mischievous smile.

"Wait. I've got something even better."

Margo

I reached into the drawer, pulling out my favorite vibrator. It was long and thick with a clit teasing attachment. I pressed the button, and a loud buzzing filled the room.

"You sure you don't want to come first?" I asked with a smile. "I'm glad to wait."

Lia flopped over onto her back.

"Well, if you insist."

With our positions reversed, I leaned over her and kissed her deeply. I'd been telling myself for two weeks that this couldn't happen. That I couldn't cross the boss boundary. That going back for seconds with my spring fling or even considering a relationship with Lia was a bad idea. But somewhere between eating pizza and watching "Encanto", I'd changed my mind.

I had a high powered job with a lot of stress. I was mostly a single parent, with a very active and extremely precocious girl. Other than that trip to Mexico, almost everything I'd done over the last several years was for someone else...my boss, my daughter, my husband.

This, this was purely for me.

Lots of single moms dated. I wasn't going to feel bad about having some adult time. Being desperate for orgasms didn't make me a bad mom.

Lia coming back into my life felt like fate or something. What were the chances that a woman I'd met on vacation, a woman who didn't even know my last name, would turn up on my porch? This had to be the universe offering us a second chance. I was damn well not going to squander this opportunity, not when the attraction between us still burned as bright as it did when I first looked over and saw her lying on the beach in a bright yellow bikini.

Sure, Amelia was technically my employee. But that was only for three months. Us getting together would be okay because our professional relationship was temporary. At least that's how I justified it to myself. Come September, Skyler would go back to school and Lia would start her teaching job.

If I played my cards right, maybe Lia would be moving in with us too. For the first time since my divorce, I was picturing someone else in my life. In my house. Helping to parent my daughter.

Maybe I was moving too fast, but it felt right.

Skyler loved Lia as much as I did. Every night when I came home from work, she told me every single thing she and Lia did that day in explicit detail. But it wasn't all fun and games with my daughter and her nanny. I'd told Lia that Skyler had been struggling with math, and without me asking her to do it, Lia had started tutoring my daughter, somehow getting her to actually enjoy doing math problems.

She was a miracle worker. But right now, there was only one miracle I wanted to work on.

I kissed Lia, my tongue tangling with hers as I moved the vibrator to circle her breasts. She moaned against my mouth, her nipples rising to hard peaks under the vibrations. When she was writhing underneath me just from me teasing her breasts, I moved down to kneel between her legs.

Her pussy was beautiful, her neat patch of pubic hair matching the red on her head. It was glistening with arousal, and when I slid my fingers between her lower lips, they came away slick.

"You're so wet already," I whispered approvingly. "Let's see if we can get you any wetter."

I pushed her legs farther apart and teased the vibrator up and down between her folds, stroking her with the vibrating head before I finally stopped and pressed the toy against her opening. I slid it in partway, then pulled it back, teasing her. I repeated the action several times, going deeper every time, until it was fully seated inside the depths of her channel.

Twisting the device, I pulled back the hood of her clit, then arranged the vibe's attachment right over the swollen bundle of nerves. I knew from experience that the little attachment was quite effective.

I could tell that Lia was already close. Her fingers were gripping the sheets, her eyes closed as she made little whining sounds. I could practically come just from watching that face she was making.

I shifted until my thigh was between hers and pressed it up against the edge of the vibe. Lowering my head, I drew one of her breasts into my mouth and started humping her thigh. With every movement, my thigh hit the vibrator, shoving it deeper inside her, then popping back out a bit when I retreated.

Lia wrapped one leg around my waist, changing the angle of her pelvis and squeezing me tight.

"Fuck, Margo, I'm so close."

I lifted my mouth from the sweetness of her tit.

"Let go," I said. "Come for me, Lia. Now."

I bit down on the closest nipple, pinching the other between my fingers, and moved my hips a little faster, grinding against the vibrator and her thigh.

Lia stiffened beneath me and apparently remembering that my daughter was in the next room, she shoved a pillow over her face, muffling the sounds of her release. Even through the fabric, I could hear her high-pitched sounds of pleasure. My girl was a screamer. I'd thought more than once that it was good we'd been in a separate cabana in Mexico; if we'd had neighbors on the other side of the wall we would have gotten noise complaints for sure.

I felt proud of how quickly I'd gotten Lia off. After so many hours learning her body when we were in Mexico, it all came back to me how to give her the maximum amount of pleasure.

As she came down from her orgasm, I switched off the vibrator and tossed it aside. I heard it hit the floor with a soft thump.

My pussy was throbbing with need, and now I was desperate to come. It had been three long months since I'd been with Lia – or anyone else – and I was close to going off just from sliding against her thigh.

Rousing herself, Lia gave me a smile.

"I'm too exhausted to move. How about you come sit on my face?"

She didn't have to ask me twice. I crawled up to kneel on either side of her head, grabbing my brass headboard as I lowered my core downward. Lia gripped my hips, maneuvering me lower. Given her bird's eye view of my pussy, I was glad I'd done some grooming recently.

I jumped when I felt the first touch of her rough tongue sliding between my folds. It felt like a little electric shock that zapped up my core.

"Lia!" I whined.

Lia's fingers tightened on my hips, and she pulled me down a bit more, her tongue spearing inside my channel, pumping in and out. I whimpered, rolling my core against her face, seeking the pressure I needed to finally get over the edge.

But Lia knew my body as well as I knew hers. One of her hands left my hips, moving to pinch my clit between two fingers. And that was all it took.

I damn near bit through my lip to keep from screaming as I fucked her face, my entire body shuddering with the force of my orgasms. I gripped the headboard so hard my fingers ached, and I could feel it thumping softly against the wall.

Moisture flooded my pussy as I ground against Lia's face, but her talented tongue moved quickly, lapping up every drop. My toes curled against her sides as wave after wave of pleasure rolled through my body.

When I was finally done, I fell to the bed next to her, completely boneless, my breath coming in heaving pants.

"Holy fuck," I whispered, feeling shellshocked.

Sex with Lia had always been good – shockingly good. But this felt like something more. It was next level good.

"I know, I feel it too," she answered softly, pulling me into her arms. "Come here, baby."

I grabbed the light comforter, drawing it to cover us so we wouldn't get chilled, then I snuggled into her side as sleep overtook me. And for the first time since I left Mexico, I felt completely content.

Amelia

When I woke up, the sun was shining in the window. I opened one eye, confused, then saw a familiar looking blonde head laying on my breast. Margo. She looked beautiful, her face flushed, her expression peaceful.

I heard the pounding of little feet, alerting me that it was late enough for Skyler to be awake. Shit. I hadn't meant to stay this late. My plan was to get up super early and go back to my place before Margo's kid woke up.

Shoving Margo to the side, I rolled off the bed, dropping to the floor just as the door opened. Silently I scooted underneath the bed.

"What the—-?" Margo's voice was thick with sleep.

"Good morning, Mommy."

"Um. Good morning, honey. How did you sleep?" She sounded confused.

"Good. Can I get pancakes for breakfast?"

"Yeah, just give Mommy a few minutes to wake up, okay? Be a good girl and set the table for me please."

"Okay."

I heard footsteps head towards the door then Margo added, "Can you close the door behind you please?"

Once the door closed, Margo's head appeared on the side of the bed.

"You didn't have to hide under the bed like a criminal," she laughed. Her hair touched the floor as she hung upside down over the edge of the bed.

I scooted out, then sat up. Noticing the vibrator was still on the floor, I handed it to Margo with a quirk of my lips. Good thing her inquisitive child hadn't seen that.

"I didn't want to give Skyler the wrong impression," I whispered. "It will be confusing for her to find me here in your room. I'll just put on my clothes and go out the window."

"Don't be ridiculous," she said. "What are you going to do? Shimmy down the drainpipe? We're on the second floor."

"Oh yeah, I forgot."

I looked around, trying to figure out another way to escape.

"Just join us for breakfast. Skyler will be thrilled that you're here. And she's too young to understand what happened anyway."

I shook my head. "She's already getting ideas about us. She was talking about how great it would be if we were girlfriends just yesterday, trying to sell me on the idea. I'm sure that's why she wanted to invite me to dinner."

"Maybe we could be," she said in a careful voice.

"Could be what?" I asked in confusion.

"Girlfriends."

A rush of emotions passed through my brain, faster than I could categorize them. I couldn't deny that the idea was appealing. I'd loved waking up with Margo in my arms this morning. I'd loved hanging out as a family last night. But this couldn't happen.

"Let's just talk later," I demurred, grabbing my bra and shirt off the floor near me and pulling them on.

Suddenly the door to the bedroom burst open again. I was still sitting on the floor, but Skyler's gaze went right to me.

"Amelia!" She sounded delighted. "I didn't know you were here! Did you and my mom have a sleepover?"

I pulled the hem of my shirt over my lap to hide my naked lower body.

"Um. Kind of."

"Mommy's making pancakes for breakfast."

"I heard."

"Pancakes are my favorite. Well, after pizza. Do you like pancakes Amelia?"

"Yeah, I do."

Margo shifted around behind us, getting dressed. She grabbed Skyler's hand. "How about you and I get started on breakfast while Lia gets dressed."

"Okay Mommy."

When they left the room, I pulled up my legs and dropped my forehead to my knees with a sigh. This was exactly what I didn't want to happen. It would be hard enough to leave Skyler when I was done being her nanny. If we crossed over to a personal relationship, it was going to be even harder for both of us when Margo and I went our separate ways. I really liked the little girl, and I had no desire to hurt her.

But the cat was out of the bag now. I might as well go have some pancakes with the Langley women. Like my little friend Skyler, pancakes were my favorite breakfast.

Against both Margo and Skyler's protests, I left right after breakfast. Skyler's dad was picking her up at ten, and I'd had enough awkwardness for one day. I didn't need to meet Margo's ex-husband on top of everything else. I wanted to get home and do some laundry. Or sit on the couch and stare at mindless television shows while I pondered my night with Margo.

I'd told myself that our vacation fling was just that, a fling. That it didn't mean anything. Yet when I fell asleep wrapped around her last night, it definitely felt like more.

The truth was, I was falling for her. Well, if I was being honest, I'd already fallen for her. I'd fallen for her way back when we were in Mexico, and my feelings had been growing ever since I'd started working for Margo, despite my best efforts. I'd tried hard to keep things professional, even while our daily conversations had slowly veered into other topics besides her daughter. Accepting Skyler's invitation to stay for dinner was a huge tactical error.

Fucking her mother? An even bigger error.

Margo was ten years older than me. She had a fancy job that required her to wear designer outfits to work. She owned a house and had a kid.

Meanwhile I was just starting my career, lived in a crappy one-bedroom apartment, drove a seventeen year old car, and picked up my clothes at thrift shops.

We couldn't be more different. And yet we seemed to fit. It wasn't just sex – although that was incredible. We also had a lot in common. Things just seemed easy between us, almost like we'd been together forever. There was no pretense between us. Even with Skyler it almost felt like we were co-parents, not nanny and employer.

I was so confused.

After ignoring Margo's multiple texts on Saturday, I went to Morning Jolt first thing Sunday morning. I'd picked up a relief shift and was working behind the counter with Hannah, the woman who'd gotten me the job.

During a quiet time at the coffee shop, somehow the topic of Margo came up. I ended up spilling the whole story.

"I don't get it," she said. "You had a great time with this woman in Mexico, and now you've found each other again like something out of a movie. You like her, you like her kid, and she likes you. What's the problem?"

"I dated a woman with a kid once," I shared. "I was so in love with this girl. In retrospect I think I liked her more than I liked the mom. Then we broke up, and it was terrible. I'd spent two years being a second parent to this little girl, and then I was totally cut off from her with no warning. I wasn't even allowed to say goodbye. It was heart-breaking."

"That's sounds hard," Hannah said sympathetically. "But that doesn't mean it will happen again. Margo doesn't seem like the vindictive type."

"I don't want to take that chance," I said firmly.

"So you're never going to date anyone with a kid?" she asked.

"Nope."

"That's too bad, because it sounds like this Margo chick really likes you."

"I'm sure she does, but how long will it last?"

"Maybe you could have had something special with this woman, but you'll never know if you're too scared to try."

Margo

"She's ghosting me."

"She can't really ghost you if she's working for you," my friend Alice pointed out. "Plus, you just saw her at breakfast yesterday morning. I'm not sure that qualifies as ghosting."

Alice was probably my best friend after my husband. We'd both come up through the ranks at Phoenix Software and we worked together closely. The two of us were one of a handful of our boss Madison's most trusted advisors. And friends.

"She hasn't answered any of my texts since then," I told Alice. "And when I call her, it goes right to voicemail."

"Maybe she needs some time to think. Or she was super busy."

"I just don't understand what happened. We woke up, she hid under the bed, we had pancakes, and then she left like her hair was on fire."

"What? She was under the bed?" Alice asked. "What kind of kinky shit did you two get up to?"

I laughed.

"Lia heard Skyler coming into my bedroom and she hid under the bed so Skyler wouldn't see her in my room buck naked," I explained. "But then after I got rid of her, Skyler came back unexpectedly and caught Lia in there anyway."

"Oops. Did Skyler freak out?"

"Not at all. Apparently my daughter had been 'shipping' us and was thrilled to hear we'd had a sleepover, even though I'm quite sure she doesn't know what that means," I explained. "She'd hang out with Lia twenty-four seven if she could. I'm pretty sure she likes Lia more than me."

"Did something happen over breakfast then that made Lia upset?"

"No. I don't think so. I mean, Skyler was there, so that was our focus. You know how she chatters on. But as soon as we'd finished eating, Lia rushed out."

I sighed deeply.

"We had such a good night together on Friday, Alice. The perfect night. It was like we were a married couple, watching movies then having hot and heavy sex as soon as the kid was in bed."

"So Mexico wasn't a fluke, huh?"

"It was not," I confirmed. "Things between us were...explosive. We both were completely satisfied. I don't know what went wrong. Maybe she thinks I'm too old for her?"

"How big is your age gap?" my friend asked.

"Ten years."

"Ah, that's nothing. Only a little bit more than me and Jewel."

Alice was in a long-term relationship with her best friend's little sister, Jewel. There was a seven year age difference between them, which was funny because when you saw them together, it was clear that Jewel was the one in charge in their relationship. But despite the gap in their ages and their very different personalities, they'd been together for a few years now, and seemed very happy.

"I'm in love with her. I knew it in Mexico, but I told myself I was being ridiculous, creating some kind of instalove fantasy. But now that I've spent more time with her, I know it's not a fantasy. I love her."

"Wow, that's big."

"What if she doesn't feel the same?" I asked, my voice small.

"Then you'll survive. It'll hurt, but it won't kill you. But maybe she just needs some time. Or something else is bothering her. You'll never know until you can talk."

I sighed deeply. "Unless she calls in sick or something, I'm going to talk to her tomorrow. Even if I have to tie her down to do it."

Unbidden, the image of Lia naked and tied to the bed came to my mind. If we got back together, we definitely needed to try that...

The next morning I was up early, nervous about what was going on with Lia. I got ready for work and paced around restlessly, until even Skyler noticed.

"What's wrong, Mommy?" she asked. "Are you upset about something? Do you have a big meeting at work?"

"I'm fine, sweetie," I reassured her with a smile. "Why don't you get your cereal? I'll keep an eye out for Lia."

Lia showed up five minutes after I was supposed to leave for work. Given that she'd never been late before, I couldn't help but wonder if she'd come late on purpose to avoid talking to me.

As she did every morning, she knocked on the door before letting herself in with her key. I was standing in the atrium waiting for her. My eyes traveled over her slim figure, taking in her baggy shorts and loose tee shirt. I wondered if she'd dressed to be as unprovocative as possible. If so, it was a useless effort. I already knew every curve of the slim body beneath the baggy clothes.

"Hey," I said, studying her face for some indication of what she was feeling.

Her expression was carefully blank.

"Good morning," she said, avoiding my gaze. "Where's Skyler?"

"She's in the kitchen, having breakfast."

"Okay, have a good day at work."

I'm not going to lie, her casual dismissal was like a knife to the heart. Lia started to walk away, and I grabbed her wrist, stopping her progress. I waited until she looked at me.

"We need to talk."

"I don't think we do." Her voice was cool. Neutral. "Besides, you need to get to work."

"I do, but I want to talk tonight when I get home," I said. "I know you want to pretend like Friday never happened, but it did, and we should talk about what it means."

"It doesn't mean anything," she snapped.

"You and I both know that's not true. Please, just give me a chance to talk to you tonight."

She pulled her hand away and headed towards the kitchen without a word.

Amelia

I felt like a shithead for how I'd treated Margo this morning. I knew I needed to suck it up and talk to her, but I just wasn't sure what I would say.

With supreme effort, I put Margo out of my mind so I could focus on Skyler. I had a job to do, and I wasn't going to neglect my little ward just because I was conflicted about her mother.

Conflicted wasn't the right word though. The real problem was that I was hopelessly, irretrievably in love with Margo. Our night together had just cemented that. And I had no clue what to do about it. I could feel my anxiety increasing the closer it got to six o'clock, knowing that Margo would be home soon.

"Mommy's home!" Skyler announced happily when she heard the door open. She raced into the living room to give Margo a hug, me following behind her at a slower pace.

"How'd it go today?" Margo asked us, as she did every day. Her words were calm, but I could tell from her face that she was nervous. That made two of us.

"Great!" Skyler said enthusiastically. "We practiced doing cartwheels, and Amelia taught me how to add up sums that are three digits like one hundred forty plus two hundred and seven. It works just like when there's two digits."

"Wow, that's cool. Good job."

Margo rubbed her hair affectionately. "Hey Sky, how about you have thirty minutes of screen time now? Lia and I need to talk about some stuff."

"Yay!" Skyler turned on her heel and rushed towards the family room, then stopped. "Can Amelia stay for dinner? You could stay in my room this time, Amelia and do your sleepover with me."

"We'll see," Margo demurred. "Go pick out your show."

Once Skyler was gone, Margo inclined her head towards the kitchen. I followed her without argument. There was no sense putting it off anymore. Things would just get more and more awkward every day.

Margo grabbed a bottle of beer from the refrigerator, offering one to me. I accepted the beer, sitting at the table. Margo sat across from me.

"Did I do something wrong?" she asked, pain etched on her face. "I thought we had a good night on Friday."

"It was good, really good," I conceded. "It's just...I don't think we should do that again."

"Why not?"

When I didn't answer right away, she continued, "We had such a great time in Mexico, but when I got home I convinced myself that I'd overinflated it. That I didn't like you as much as I thought I did. But when we were together Friday I realized, what we have is real. At least it is for me."

I rubbed my hand on my chest, trying to soothe the aching.

"I can't have a relationship with you, Margo."

"May I ask why?"

"You have a daughter."

"So? I thought you liked Skyler."

"I love her, that's the problem."

She frowned. "I don't understand."

"I dated a woman with a kid before. I was totally in love with that little girl, but then she was torn away from me," I explained. "My ex wouldn't even let me say goodbye. It broke my heart. Losing that kid was worse than losing my girlfriend. I heard from mutual friends that it was devastating for her, she didn't understand why I'd abandoned her. She was so upset she started acting up in school."

I leaned forward, wrapping my hand around Margo's on the table.

"Don't you see?" My tone was anguished. "If things don't work out between us, I don't just lose you, I lose Skyler. And the one who will be hurt the most is that little girl in there watching Encanto for the seven hundredth time."

Margo's eyes filled with tears. "You don't want to be with me because you're afraid of hurting my daughter?" she asked. "I can't decide if that's the sweetest thing I've ever heard, or the most ridiculous."

She put her other hand on top of mine, trapping my hand between hers, and gave me a little squeeze.

"I'm in love with you," she said. "Maybe it's crazy, but I knew it in Mexico. It was confirmed for me the minute I saw you on my porch talking to my daughter. And it's only grown over this last month. I love you and I want to spend the rest of my life with you, Lia. But if for some crazy reason it doesn't work out, I promise I'll give Skyler the option of still seeing you."

She paused. "Well, unless you commit a crime or something. I'm not going to let my little girl visit you in prison or rehab."

I rolled my eyes. "I just passed a background check for my teaching job. I've never committed a crime or done drugs in my life, not even marijuana. If that makes you feel any better."

She smirked. "It totally does."

We stared at each other for a long moment before I spoke, deciding to share what was in my heart, even though it was a huge risk.

"I love you too, Margo."

Her eyes lit up. "You do?"

"Yeah. I love you and Skyler both."

"That's good, since we love you too. I speak with authority, since Skyler tells me about ten times a day how awesome you are."

Releasing my hand, Margo stood up and walked to my chair, grabbing the back to rotate it away from the table. Throwing her leg over mine, she straddled my lap, her inner thighs pressed tight against my outer thighs.

Bringing her hands to my shoulders, she leaned in until I could feel her breath on my lips.

"Will you stay over tonight?"

I pretended to consider her invitation. "I don't know, can you be quiet while I make you come your brains out?"

"I can try."

"Will there be pancakes?"

"Only on weekends."

"I don't know then. The pancakes are kind of a deal breaker."

She leaned forward, her lips capturing mine, and kissed me deeply. I wrapped my hands around her ass, squeezing her cheeks as I pulled her closer. Our upper bodies pressed against each other as we poured all of our emotions into the kiss.

Margo rubbed her breasts against mine, ramping up my excitement. We were so focused on our kiss that we didn't hear Skyler come in until she squealed, "You're kissing! Does this mean we're having another sleepover?"

Margo pulled away with a smirk. "Welcome to parenthood. Hope you don't mind never having any privacy."

"I don't need privacy if I'm with you," I whispered.

"And me!" Skyler added.

Epilogue – Margo

Eleven months later...

"Yay, we're done with school!"

Skyler tossed her backpack on the floor, throwing up her hands in triumph. Lia walked in right behind her, dropping her briefcase next to Skyler's bag.

"Yay, we're done with school!" Lia echoed.

I'd left work early today to get Skyler ready to go to her father's. My ex was taking her for a week to visit her grandparents in Colorado. Meanwhile, Lia and I were heading back to Mexico, visiting the same all-inclusive resort where we met about fifteen months ago.

We hustled through gathering Skyler's half-packed suitcase, doubled checked that she had all of her most important toys, and after a long goodbye, packed her up in the back of her father's Subaru. I'd miss her of course, but I was also looking forward to spending an uninterrupted week of alone time with the woman I loved.

I had a ring tucked away in my suitcase, and I couldn't wait to make things official with Lia. More official, since she'd moved in with us at the end of last summer, as soon as her nanny gig was over.

Things between us had been great, better than I could have hoped. Our lives had all meshed seamlessly and I'd be lying if I said I didn't appreciate having another adult in the house to help with things like housework and entertaining Skyler.

But mostly, I loved the closeness of having a companion, someone who loved me, and who let me love them back. Although the sex was nothing to shake a stick at either. We were still as insatiable as we'd been in Mexico.

I closed the front door to find Lia staring at me, her hands behind her back. She looked nervous.

"What's wrong?" I asked. I couldn't imagine what had happened in the three minutes I'd been outside saying goodbye to Skyler.

She stepped closer. "Nothing, it's just that...well..."

Lia dropped to her knees, then drew her hands back in front of her, a dark blue ring box on her palm.

"Margo, love, would you marry me?"

I pressed my hand against my mouth, staring at the box in her hand, my eyes filling with tears.

Apparently I stared too long, because after a few seconds, Lia started to look uncomfortable.

"Is it too soon?" she asked.

I shook my head. Grabbing her wrist, I pulled her to standing.

"Come with me."

Tugging her behind me, I led her into the bedroom, then opened up my suitcase, digging out the ring I'd hidden in the toe of one of my shoes. I held the ring box out to her. It was the same color as the box in Lia's hands.

Her eyes widened in surprise.

"I'll marry you if you marry me," I said, pressing the ring box into her hand.

She handed me my velvet box and we both opened them together, gasping as we viewed the different rings that we'd picked out for each other.

"It's beautiful," Lia said as she slid her ring onto the third finger of her left hand.

"I love it," I said as I did the same, noting how the ring fit my finger perfectly.

We put our hands out side by side, admiring the rings we'd each gotten from the other.

"I guess it's true that great minds think alike," Lia said.

"And I guess it's true that love will always find a way."

She rolled her eyes at my corny statement, but pulled me into her arms, her lips hovering near mine.

"How about we celebrate before we finish packing?"

***

Check out the story of how Margo's friend Alice got together with a younger woman named Jewel in "My BFF's Sister[1]" and read about barista Hannah's relationship with her business woman in "My Holiday Love[2]". Both are available now at all major retailers.

If you liked this book, please consider leaving a review or rating to let me know. You can find more of Reba's lesbian romances on her website at Books2read.com/rl/lesbianromance[3]

Be sure to join my newsletter for more great books. You'll receive a free book when you join my newsletter. Subscribers are the first to hear about all of my new releases and sales. Visit my mailing list sign-up at bit.ly/rebabooks[4] to download your free book today.

---

1. https://books2read.com/u/4NxD1J

2. https://books2read.com/MyHolidayLove

3. *https://books2read.com/rl/lesbianromance*

4.   https://bit.ly/rebabooks

Special Preview

The Divorcee's First Time
A Contemporary Lesbian Romance
By Reba Bale

"It's done," I said triumphantly. "My divorce is final."

My best friend Susan paused in the process of sliding into the restaurant booth, her sharply manicured eyebrows raising almost to her hairline. "Dickhead finally signed the papers?" she asked, her tone hopeful.

I nodded as Susan settled into the seat across from me. "The judge signed off on it today. Apparently his barely legal girlfriend is knocked up, and she wants to get a ring on her finger before the big event." I explained with a touch of irony in my voice. "The child bride finally got it done for me."

Susan smiled and nodded. "Well congratulations and good riddance. Let's order some wine."

We were most of the way through our second bottle when the conversation turned back to my ex. "I wonder if Dickhead and his Child Bride will last for the long haul," Susan mused.

I shook my head and blew a chunk of hair away from my mouth.

"I doubt it," I told her. "Someday she's gonna roll over and think, there's got to be something better out there than a self-absorbed man child who doesn't know a clitoris from a doorknob."

Susan laughed, sputtering her wine. I eyed her across the table. Although she was ten years older than me, we had been best friends for the last five years. We worked together at the accounting firm. She had been my trainer when I first came there, fresh out of school with my degree. We bonded over work, but soon realized that we were kindred spirits.

Susan was rapidly approaching forty but could easily pass for my age. Her hair was black and shiny, hinting at her Puerto Rican heritage, with blunt bangs and blond highlights that she paid a fortune for. Her face was clear and unlined, with large brown eyes and cheek bones that could cut glass. She was an avid runner and worked hard to maintain a slim physique since the women in her family ran towards the chunkier side.

I was almost her complete opposite. Blonde curls to her straight dark hair, blue eyes instead of brown, curvy where she was lean, introverted to her extrovert.

But somehow, we clicked. We were closer than sisters. Honestly, I don't know how I would have gotten through the last year without her. She had been the first one I called when my marriage fell apart, and she had supported me throughout the whole process.

It had been a big shock when I came home early one day and found my husband getting a blow job in the middle of our living room. It had been even more shocking when I saw the fresh young face at the other end of that blow job.

"What the fuck are you doing?" I had screeched, startling them both out of their sex stupor. "You're getting blow jobs from children now?"

The girl had looked up from her knees with eyes glowing in righteous indignation. "I'm not a child, I'm nineteen," she had informed me proudly. "I'm glad you finally found out. I give him what you don't, and he loves me."

I looked into the familiar eyes of my husband and saw the panic and confusion there. I made it easy for him. "Get out," I told him firmly, my voice leaving no room for argument. "Take your teenage girlfriend and get the fuck out. We're getting a divorce. Expect to hear from my lawyer."

The condo was in my name. I had purchased it before we were married, and since I had never added his name to the deed, he had no rights to it. There was no question he would be the one leaving.

My husband just stared at me with his jaw hanging open like he couldn't believe it. "But Jennifer," he whined. "You don't understand. Let me explain."

"There's nothing to understand," I told him sadly. "This is a deal breaker for me, and you know that as well as I do. We are done."

The girl had taken his hand and smiled triumphantly. "Come on baby," she told him. "Zip up and let's get out of here. We can finally be together like we planned."

"Yeah baby," I had sneered. "I'll box up your stuff. It'll be in the hallway tomorrow. Pick it up by six o'clock or I'm trashing it all."

After they left my first call was to the locksmith, but my second call was to Susan.

That night was the last time I had seen my husband until we had met for the court-ordered pre-divorce mediation. He spent most of that session reiterating what he had told me in numerous voice mails, emails and sessions spent yelling on the other side of my front door. He loved me. He had made a terrible mistake. He wasn't going to sign the papers. We were meant to be together. Needless to say, mediation hadn't been very successful. Fortunately, I had been careful to keep our assets separate, as if I knew that someday I would be in this situation.

Through it all, Susan had been my rock. In the end I don't think I was even that sad about the divorce, I was really angrier with myself for staying in a relationship that wasn't fulfilling with a man I didn't love anymore.

"You need to get some quality sex." Susan drew my attention back to the present. "Bang him out of your system."

"I don't know," I answered slowly. "I think I need a hiatus."

"A hiatus from what?" Susan asked with a frown. "You haven't had sex in what, eighteen months?"

I nodded. "Yeah, but I just can't take a disappointing fumble right now. I would rather have nothing than another three-pump chump."

I shook my head and continued, "I'm going to stick with my battery-operated boyfriend, he never disappoints me."

Susan smiled. "That's because you know your way around your own vajayjay."

She motioned to the waiter to bring us a third bottle of wine.

"That's why I like to date women," she continued. "We already know our way around the equipment."

I nodded thoughtfully. "You make a good point."

Susan leaned forward. "We've never talked about this," she said earnestly. "Have you ever been with a woman?"

For more of the story, check out "The Divorcee's First Time" by Reba Bale, available for immediate download[1] today.

***

Want a free book? Join my newsletter and a special gift. I'll contact you a few times a month with story updates, new releases, and special sales. Visit bit.ly/rebababooks[2] for more information.

---

1.   **https://books2read.com/u/bpznKX**

2. https://bit.ly/rebabooks

Other Books by Reba Bale

Check out my other books, available on most major online retailers now. Go to my webpage[1] at bit.ly/AuthorRebaBale to learn more.

Friends to Lovers Lesbian Romance Series

The Divorcee's First Time
My BFF's Sister
My Rockstar Assistant
My College Crush
My Fake Girlfriend
My Secret Crush
My Holiday Love
My Valentine's Gift
My Spring Fling
Coming Out in Ten Dates

Menage Romances

Pie Promises
Tornado Warning
Summer in Paradise
Life of the Mardi

Hotwife Erotic Romances

Hotwife in the Woods
Hotwife on the Beach
Hotwife Under the Tree
A Hotwife's Retreat
Hot Wife Happy Life

The Marriage Survival Series

Finding His Alpha: A Wife's First Spanking

---

1. https://books2read.com/ap/nB2qJv/Reba-Bale

Watching His Wife: The First Time Sharing

Exploring His Fantasy: A First Time Gay Ménage

The Divorce Recovery Series

Spanking Justice: A Middle-Aged Divorcee's First Spanking

A Punishing Workout: Spanked by the Trainer

A Disciplined Budget: Spanked by the Accountant

The Spanking Therapy Series

The Reluctant Bride's First Spanking

The Reluctant Bride Gets Caught

The Billionaire Gets Punished

The Curvy Reporter Gets Punished

Unlikely Doms Series

Alpha in a Sweater Vest

Alpha Plumber

Hotel Spanking

Alpha Student

Alpha Yogi

The Voyeur Romance Series

Naughty Sunbathing

Naughty Dinner Date

Naughty Laundry Date

Naughty Camping

Paying for Tuition

The Babysitter's Ride Home

The Babysitter's First Menage

The Teaching Assistant's Lesson

The Billionaire's Assistant

Toys for Grown-Ups Series

Financial Punishment

Menage a Geek

Punishing Holidays

Turkey and a Spanking
Shopping and a Spanking
Other Standalone Stories
Sinful Desires
The Ride of My Life
Taken by Surprise
Share Me: A Cheating Husband's Punishment
Want a free book? Just join my newsletter at bit.ly/rebabooks[2]! You'll be the first to hear about new releases, special sales, and free offers.

---

2. *https://bit.ly/rebabooks*

About the Author

Reba Bale loves writing naughty stories where the characters are able to tap into their inner fantasies and experience spanking, bondage, humiliation, or other activities on the non-vanilla side of life. When Reba is not writing she is reading the same naughty stories she likes to write.

You can also follow Reba on Medium[3] for free stories, bonus epilogues and more. You can also hear all about new releases and special sales by joining Reba's newsletter mailing list.[4]

---

3.   https://medium.com/@authorrebabale

4.   https://bit.ly/rebabooks

Don't miss out!

Visit the website below and you can sign up to receive emails whenever Reba Bale publishes a new book. There's no charge and no obligation.

https://books2read.com/r/B-A-IDTM-AKNFC

BOOKS 2 READ

Connecting independent readers to independent writers.

Did you love *My Spring Fling*? Then you should read *My BFF's Sister*[5] by Reba Bale!

Her best friend's sister is strictly off-limits, especially when her friend has no idea that her little sister is a lesbian.

Jewel is back from a long stint in the Peace Corps and ready to start her new life back in her hometown. She's ready to come out to her family and live life without apology. A chance encounter with her sister's best friend Alice brings back memories of her childhood crush. Alice still sees her as the pesky kid sister, but Jewel is all grown up now and knows exactly how to take what she wants – and she wants Alice.

Can Jewel convince Alice to take a chance on love, even if it may destroy her longest friendship?

---

5. https://books2read.com/u/4NxD1J

6. https://books2read.com/u/4NxD1J

"My BFF's Sister" is book two in the "Friends to Lovers" romantic novella series. Each book in the series is a steamy standalone featuring an LGBTQ couple making the leap from friends to lovers. This book includes explicit sexual activity between consenting adults. It is intended for mature audiences only.